JIM ARNOSKY

Turtle in the Sea

G. P. PUTNAM'S SONS · NEW YORK

Library of Congress Cataloging-in-Publication Data
Arnosky, Jim. Turtle in the sea / Jim Arnosky.   p. cm.
Summary: A turtle emerges from the sea to lay her eggs in the sand. 1. Sea turtles—Juvenile fiction.
[1. Sea turtles—Fiction. 2. Turtles—Fiction.] I. Title. PZ10.3.A86923 Tu 2002 [E]—dc21 2001048123
ISBN 0-399-22757-1
1 3 5 7 9 10 8 6 4 2
First Impression

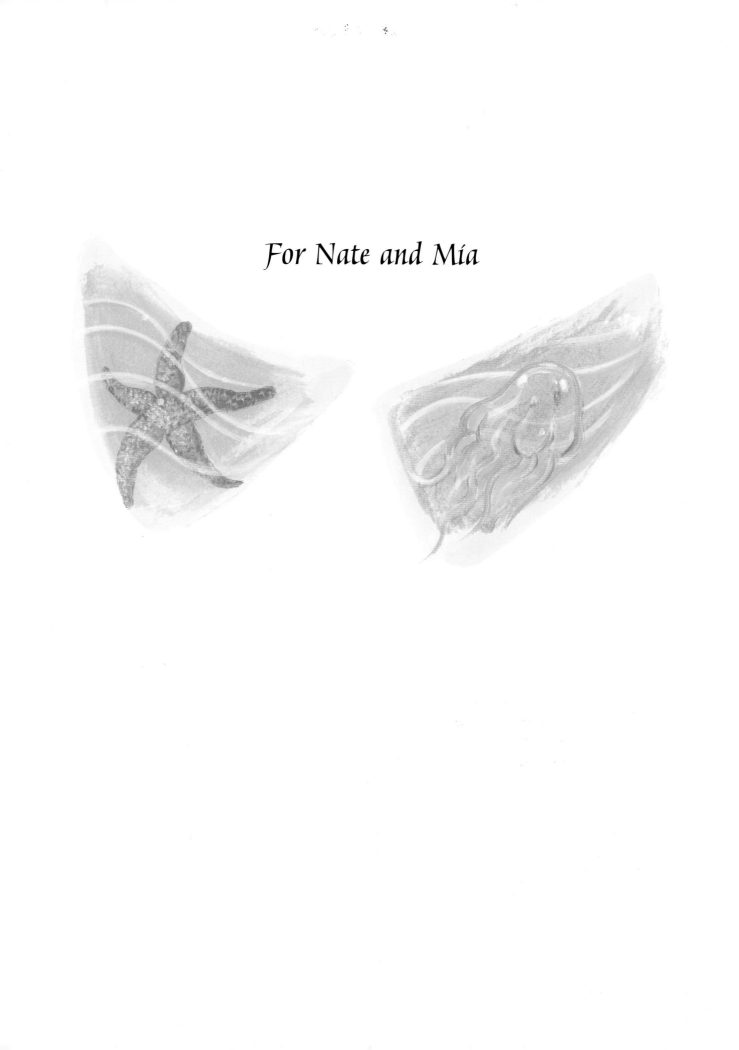

For Nate and Mía

Somewhere in the salty sea
beneath the blue-green waves,
a turtle flies in a water sky.

She is swimming to the shore.
It is time for her to dig a hole in sand
and bury her soft white turtle eggs.

She is old and large and heavy.
It is midnight when she finally
drags herself on the beach
to dry, loose sand where she can dig.

In a lighthouse beam,
the many marks and scars
of a long life in the sea
shine brightly on her shell.

Long ago, when she was young,
she was drifting lazily in the sun
above the coral reef,

when suddenly a shark
swam up and attacked her
from beneath!

3

The shark bit her shell,
but she escaped by diving
and hiding in a coral cave.
There she stayed, holding her breath
until the shark finally swam away.
Her shell was scarred.
Her back was sore.
She never again drifted
on the surface close to shore.

4

But she quickly learned that danger
also lurked in deeper water.
Late one day, in a deep channel,
where big ships made their way to sea,
she was catching jellyfish, her favorite food.

The turtle chased
one jellyfish
right into the path
of an oncoming boat,
and was plowed under
by the vessel's massive bow.

With her shell cracked and broken,
she swam to a small cove.
And there, far away
from the channel and the boats,
in peace and quiet,
she rested many days
and slowly healed.

She was way out in the ocean
when she saw the waterspout.
She didn't know it was a storm.

She watched it come closer and closer,
spinning and churning
across the dark blue waves.

Before she could dive to safety,
she was caught up in the swirling water . . .

. . . and dropped back down into a raging sea
that tumbled her and tossed her
until she washed up on the beach.

After the storm,
nicked and scratched all over
by sharp-edged bits of broken seashells,
she crawled back into the sea.
She was hungry.
She searched the murky water
for a fish
to catch and eat.

When she saw some
swimming close together,
she lunged into the bunch.
She didn't see the net.

9

Suddenly the fish net closed around her.
She felt the pulling strings,
and in a rush of bubbles and sunlight,
she was yanked up out of the water.

10

But the fisherman was kind.
He took his fish.
Then, gently, he untangled
the turtle from his net
and let her go.

She survived it all—the sharks,
the boats, the storms and nets—
in her long life swimming in the sea.

And now onshore, as she has done
so many times before, she lays her eggs
one by one, and covers them all with sand.

But she will not stay to see them hatch.
That is the turtle way.

The sun will mother them with warmth.
The sand will keep them safe.
The hatchlings
will climb up
and quickly crawl
to waves and surf.

Tiny flippers to propel them.
Tiny shells protecting.
Tiny eyes to see their world.

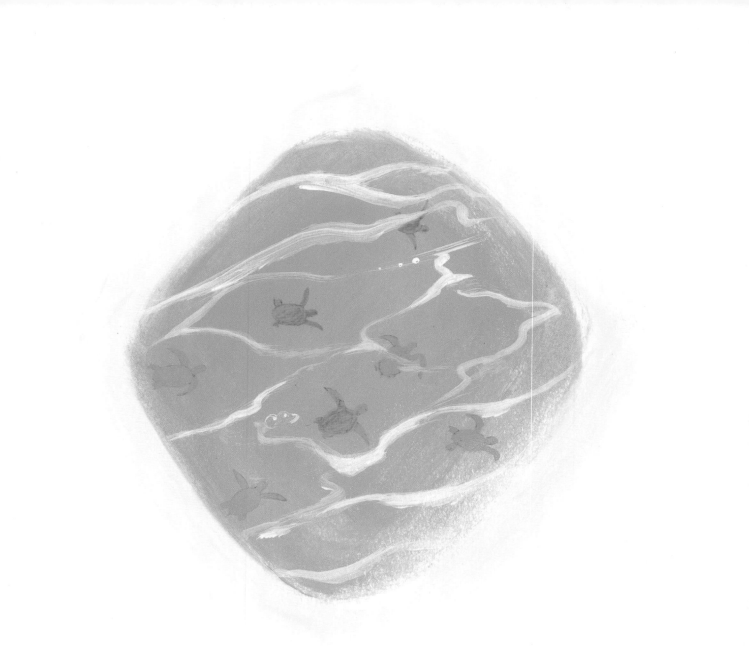

Tiny turtles in the sea.